This igloo book belongs to:

igloobooks

Published in 2015
by Igloo Books Ltd
Cottage Farm
Sywell
NN6 0BJ
www.igloobooks.com

HUN001 0115
2 4 6 8 10 9 7 5 3 1
ISBN 9781-78440-211-2

Printed and manufactured in China

I Love You This Much

igloobooks

When the weather is cloudy, if there's just one thing I could do, it would be to float up in the sky and bring sunshine home to you.

My cake would be big and tall and
covered in lovely, pink cream.
It would be a yummy, scrummy,
sticky, sweetie-licking dream.

I would do anything to cheer you up when you're feeling down.
I'd put on a funny show for you and dress up as a clown.

I'd get my friends to dress up in a silly, circus style.
Then I'd wobble on a tightrope, just to try and make you smile.

I would run through the meadows, where the wild flowers grow.
Then I'd pick the best ones for you, in the soft evening glow.

I'd whoosh over the city, across the mountains and the sea.
When I finally reach you, you'd get a super-hug from me.

I love you so much, I would gather clouds to make a lovely bed,
with the warmest fluffy blanket and a pillow for your head.

I'd imagine you were with me and ready for a rest.
Then I'd read you all the stories that I know you'd like the best

To show you how much I love you,
I'd climb a ladder to the sky.
It would reach past clouds and
sunbeams and rainbows way up high.

My ladder would stretch up to the
stars and they would shine so bright.
I'd bring the biggest one back for you,
to twinkle through the night.

I'd go up to the mountain top and shout so everyone could hear. Then I'd run back down to whisper, "I love you," in your ear.

I want to tell the world just how special you are to me,
and that when I'm with you, I'm as happy as can be.

I love you so much because I think that you're the very best.
You're all warm and cuddly and much snugglier than the rest.

I can think of lots of ways to tell you how lovely you are.
To let you know what you mean to me and
that you're my shining star.

I'm so lucky that I have you and you'll always have me, too.
I love you more than anyone, just because you're you!